Wetlands

Yvonne Franklin

Wetlands

Publishing Credits

Editorial Director
Dona Herweck Rice

Creative Director
Lee Aucoin

Associate Editor
James Anderson

Illustration Manager
Timothy J. Bradley

Editor-in-Chief
Sharon Coan, M.S.Ed.

Publisher
Rachelle Cracchiolo, M.S.Ed.

Science Consultants

Scot Oschman, Ph.D.
David W. Schroeder, M.S.

Teacher Created Materials

5301 Oceanus Drive
Huntington Beach, CA 92649-1030
http://www.tcmpub.com
ISBN 978-1-4333-0316-6

Table of Contents

A World of Their Own

Look around and listen. Fingers of land stretch into the water. Plants sprout from below the surface of the water. A dragonfly flits through the air. Thin reeds bend under the weight of tiny snails. A green frog catches a lazy fly. Blackbirds sing. Cattails bob in the wind. A heron stands on one of its long legs. It rises above the water. Below, tiny bacteria (bak-TEER-ee-uh) keep the water clean.

This is a **wetland**.

Wetlands

A wetland is an area of land that is flooded with water most of the year. Water systems and earth systems live together. Plants and animals make use of both the water and earth. Many different **species** (SPEE-seez) can be found in wetlands.

How Much?

About six percent of Earth's surface is wetlands.

A wetland has a variety of plant and animal life.

Putting the Puzzle Together

Have you ever solved a puzzle? All the pieces work together. They make a whole scene. If one piece is missing, the puzzle does not work. It needs all its pieces.

A wetland is a type of **ecosystem** (EK-oh-sis-tuhm). An ecosystem is like a puzzle. Everything lives and works together. Plants and animals depend on one another. They depend on the land, air, and water, too. They make a perfect team. It does not work well if one "piece" is missing. The puzzle is not complete.

Some parts of an ecosystem are living. Some are not. The air is not alive. But the plants and animals need it. The water and land are not alive. But the plants and animals need these, too.

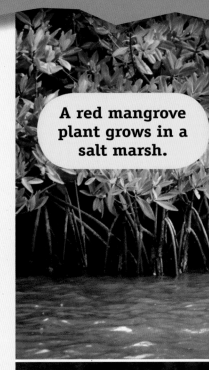

A red mangrove plant grows in a salt marsh.

Fish seek safety and food among the red mangrove's roots.

Ecosystem

The word *ecosystem* was first used in 1930. A scientist named Roy Clapham used it to describe the physical (land, air, water) and biological (plants, animals) parts of an **environment**.

Wetland Types

Swamps, bogs, and marshes are common wetlands. Estuaries, tidal pools, bayous, and vernal pools are also wetlands. Wetlands come in two types. **Freshwater wetlands** are inland. They do not have saltwater from the ocean. **Tidal wetlands** are created by ocean tides. They do have saltwater.

There is a balance of life in an ecosystem.

Disappearing Wetlands

In the United States alone, more than half the wetlands have been destroyed because of the actions of people. In the state of California, more than 90 percent of the wetlands are gone.

When wetlands are drained, the environment suffers.

Wetlands are an important part of the environment (en-VY-run-munt). But people did not always think so. They thought the wetlands were a problem. Mosquitoes (muh-SKEE-tohs) lived there. Wetlands seemed to make people ill. They thought the wetlands were a waste of land. They wanted to use the land for other things. So, people began to drain the land. They used it for farms and houses. The mosquitoes went away. The plants and animals were gone.

But the world needs wetlands. Today, people know that this is true.

Where Does the Water Come From?

Freshwater wetlands get their water from streams and rising **groundwater**. Tidal wetlands get their water there, too. But they also get it from oceans.

Wetlands are important. They act as filters for the environment. A filter lets good things through and gets rid of bad things. Wetlands filter waste from water. They keep waste from harming other living things. Of course, wetlands can only filter so much waste. If people are careless, wetlands cannot do their job.

Wetlands also hold excess water. There is a chance of floods in a heavy rain. But wetlands can keep the water from flooding other areas. They give the water time to seep into the earth or flow into the ocean.

Wetlands also make a home for living things. Plants and animals of all kinds live there. There are almost more species of animals in wetlands than in any other ecosystem.

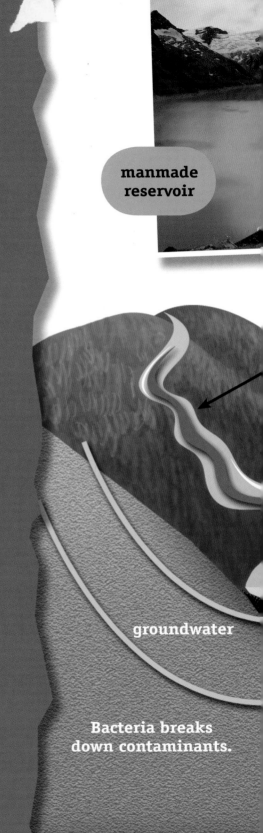

manmade reservoir

groundwater

Bacteria breaks down contaminants.

How Wetlands Work

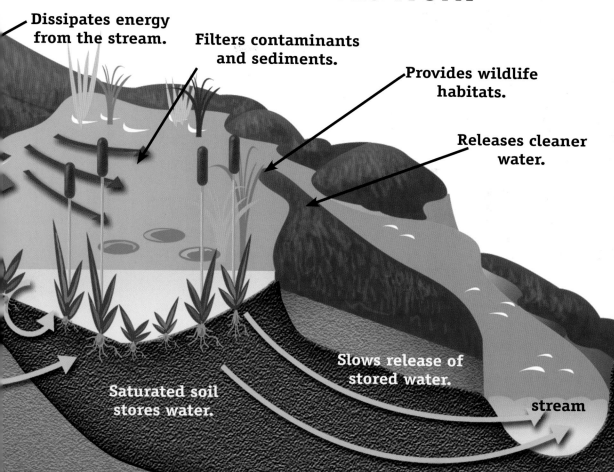

Dissipates energy from the stream.

Filters contaminants and sediments.

Provides wildlife habitats.

Releases cleaner water.

Slows release of stored water.

Saturated soil stores water.

stream

Wetland Animals

newt

river otter

grebe

Animals are an important part of most wetlands. Many species live there. **Waterfowl** are common in wetlands. So are fish and other water dwellers. Insects roam the wetlands. Spiders do, too. **Amphibians** (am-FIB-ee-uhns) such as newts are common in wetlands. So are **reptiles**. Some **mammals**, such as river otters, also make their homes there.

People often think of birds when they think of wetlands. That is because many birds live among the plants there. Most of these birds are waterbirds. Ducks swim among the waters. Geese fly over the land in the shape of a V. Herons stand on one leg in the water. Plovers dive into the water looking for fish. Grebes swim well but often fall over when running. Their feet are far back on their bodies. That makes running hard to do! Coots swim and run well. Their strong legs make it easy.

Endangered Birds

About half of all endangered bird species make their homes in wetlands.

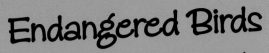

The whooping crane is an endangered species.

Water by the Gallon

Just one acre of wetlands can store about 360,000 gallons of water. (That's enough water to fill about 20 large swimming pools.) So much water makes wetlands a fun place for people to swim, boat, and play in.

After resting in a wetland, large flocks of birds take off all at once.

Birds are able to live well in wetlands. The large supply of food and water make the wetlands a good home for them. The tall plants give shelter and safety. You do not have to look far to find a bird's nest in a wetland!

With so much water, of course there are many fish there, too. Flounder, sea trout, and striped bass are common. Shrimp, clams, and crabs live there by the millions. People can make a good living fishing in the wetlands.

Insects of all kinds live in the wetlands. Wetland conditions are often just right for them. Dragonflies are very common. So are mosquitoes. Water striders may be the most interesting bugs there. They can stand on water! Tiny hairs on their legs help to keep them afloat.

Mosquito Fish

Mosquito fish help to control the large population of mosquitoes that are found in wetlands. But sometimes these fish are not native to an area. Some people may want to introduce them to new areas. This will help to keep the mosquito population low. But scientists think it is a bad idea to introduce a new species to an environment. That can disturb an ecosystem.

water strider

striped bass

freshwater shrimp

tree
frog

Frogs may be the most common amphibians in wetlands. Their croaks can echo like a chorus across the water. Crocodiles and alligators are common in wetlands. They need both land and water to live. But they are not amphibians. They are reptiles.

Many mammals can be found in wetlands. For example, muskrats are wetlands mammals. But often mammals just come to the wetlands to find prey. The wetlands may not be their home, but they could not live without them.

beaver
dam

Mammals

Mammals are warm-blooded animals with fur. They give birth to live young.

muskrat

Beavers

Beavers are the only species other than humans that can create their own wetlands! They do it by making dams and filling an area with water.

crocodile

alligator

Crocodiles and alligators have a lot in common. The biggest physical difference is in their snouts. The crocodile's is long, narrow, and V-shaped. The alligator's is shorter and U-shaped.

Wetland Plants

Every plant needs water some of the time. Wetland plants need water all of the time. One of those plants is a bulrush.

Bulrushes grow in the water in many wetlands. They are green and thin. They look similar to grass. But they are very tall. Many are taller than most people! They make a very good place for animals to live. Birds can hide their nests among the bulrushes. You can tell a bulrush by its flowers. They are shaggy and red-brown in color.

Cattails make good hiding places, too. They grow thickly in many wetlands. They can grow even taller than bulrushes do. You can spot a cattail by its long brown flowers. They look like hot dogs on the ends of skinny stalks! The flowers pop open in the fall. Their fluffy seeds float on the wind.

Las Cienegas

The Spanish word for wetland is *cienega* (see-EN-uh-guh). There is a famous street in Los Angeles that is called La Cienega. It was named for the wetlands the Spanish found when they first came to the area.

Cattails provide food and shelter for some of the animals that live in wetlands.

Reeds and rushes, like this bulrush, are common in wetlands. They grow in thick patches at the water's edge.

Oh, That Smell!

The smell from skunk cabbage attracts insects such as bees. The insects **pollinate** (POL-uh-neyt) the plant and help it to grow. But the smell probably keeps away other animals so they do not eat the plant.

Skunk cabbage can make its own heat. In this way, it can push its blooms up through frozen ground.

Some people complain of a bad smell in wetlands. It could be skunk cabbage that they smell. Skunk cabbage is a plant that grows low to the ground. It gets its name from its awful skunk-like smell. It blooms in the spring. Only its flowers can be seen then. Its leaves push up through the mud later.

The roots of the skunk cabbage pull the plant stem downward. So old plants grow deep into the earth. It is very hard to dig up an old skunk cabbage.

One of the most common types of trees in wetlands is the willow. Willows grow about 15 meters (50 feet) tall. They come in many types. You can tell each type by its leaves and branches. The weeping willow hangs its long branches low to the ground. Its leaves are pale on one side. The leaves of the pussy willow are narrow. The tree is covered in spring and summer with fluffy white blooms.

y willow
ooms

The flowers of willow trees are called catkins.

weeping willow trees

red willow bushes

Tree or Bush?

Some willows are trees and some are bushes. The main difference between a tree and a bush is in the number of stems it has. A tree usually has one. A bush usually has many. The stems of trees usually grow thicker than the stems of bushes do.

Living Together

Members of a species live together. They eat together. They have **offspring** together. Each member has a job to do. For example, a family of ducks lives together. The adults find food for the family. They also protect their offspring. The ducklings learn these skills from their parents. One day they can find food and protect their own families.

Different species live together, too. For example, certain birds live with hippos in African wetlands. The birds eat bugs that may be harmful to the hippos.

The plants and animals in an ecosystem affect each other. Some animals eat other animals. Some animals eat plants. Some plants eat animals! The Venus flytrap is like that. It east insects and spiders.

The weather in an area also affects the living things. So does the type of land, water, and air. Each part affects the other parts. Some things can survive in some conditions. Other things cannot. A polar bear could not live in a wetland. A willow tree could not live in the Arctic.

Venus flytrap

turtle and cormorant

frog in the grass

egrets fishing

Earth is made of systems that connect to each other. Every living thing is part of a system. Every nonliving thing is, too. Everything affects its environment.

Some people say that a flap of a butterfly's wing can make a tidal wave. They mean that one small action can have a big affect someplace else. People should be careful about what they do. Everything they do has an effect on everything around them. The truth is that Earth is really one big ecosystem!

fiddleheads on a woodland fern

Lab: What Makes an Ecosystem?

An ecosystem is made of relationships. Land, water, air, and living things live together. The living things depend on everything around them to survive. Do the lab activity on this page to learn more about ecosystems.

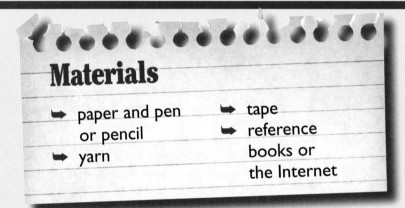

Materials

➡ paper and pen or pencil
➡ yarn
➡ tape
➡ reference books or the Internet

Procedure:

1. Copy the chart from this page onto your paper. Be sure to draw the chart on a large sheet of paper. It should be much larger than what you see here.

2. Write the name of the ecosystem at the top of the chart.

3. In each circle, write the name of something that belongs to that group that lives in the ecosystem.

4. Draw lines from each item, connecting it to every other item that it needs or uses or that needs or uses it.

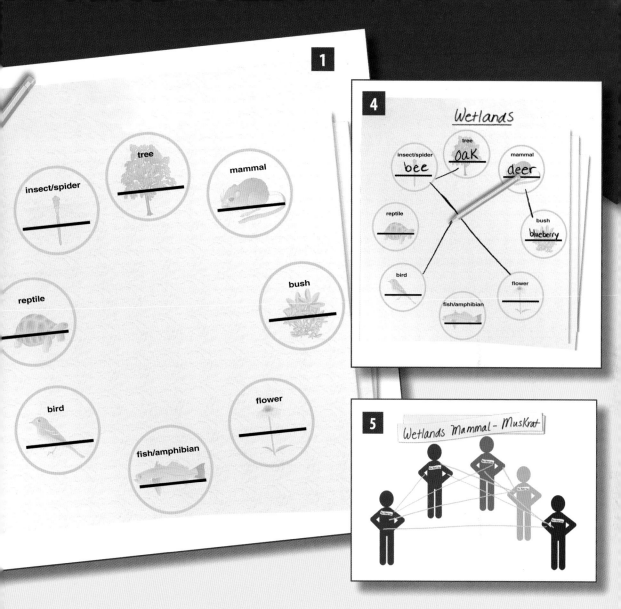

5. Now, as a class, select one of the charts that were made. You will all work together to recreate the chart in a physical way. To do it, write the key terms from the chosen chart on sentence strips and pass them out to individual students. The students now represent those key terms. Then yarn and tape can be used to connect the students. The yarn represents the lines that were connected on the chart.

6. Looking at the classroom chart, what conclusions can you make about the ecosystem? Bonus question: What part do people play in this ecosystem?

Glossary

amphibian—a cold-blooded vertebrate that lives on both water and land during its lifetime, such as a frog or toad

ecosystem— a geographical area where plants, animals, land, air, and water all interact together

environment—the air, water, minerals, living things, and everything else surrounding an area or organism

freshwater wetlands—wetlands created by water that is not salted

groundwater—water beneath the surface of the ground that can rise to the surface

mammal—a warm-blooded animal that gives birth to live young

offspring—the children or young of a particular parent

pollinate—to bring pollen to a flower

reptile—a cold-blooded vertebrate such as turtles, snakes, and crocodiles

reservoir—a natural or person-made area that holds and stores water

species—a group of living things with common characteristics or of the same type

tidal wetlands—wetlands created by salt water from the ocean tides

waterfowl—birds that live in or near the water

wetlands—an area of land that is covered in a low level of water most of the year, and in which water systems and earth systems exist together

Index

Scientists Then and Now

Rachel Carson
(1907–1964)

Mary L. Cleave
(1947–)

Rachel Carson spent a lot of time in nature when she was a girl. She also liked to read and write stories. When she grew up, she wrote about nature. Her most famous book is called *Silent Spring*. It tells how pollution can harm living things. Rachel Carson helped people to see how important it is to take care of our planet.

Mary Cleave is an expert in many areas of science. In school, she studied biology, ecology, and engineering. She spent a lot of time after college studying animals in nature. She especially did research on the desert and its animals. Then, in 1980, she became a NASA astronaut! She flew into outer space on two different space shuttle missions.